Little Donkey Learns to Help

Claude Clément
Adapted by Patricia Jensen
Illustrations by Pascal Robin

Reader's Digest Kids
Pleasantville, N.Y.—Montreal

Little Donkey was a friendly animal who liked to spend his days playing in the fields, chasing butterflies, and taking long, long naps in the sun. He was a very happy donkey, and he always did exactly as he pleased—which sometimes annoyed his friends.

One night as Little Donkey got ready for bed, his friend the sheep asked, "Little Donkey, would you please sing me a little song? I've had a very busy day, and now I'm having trouble falling asleep. I know one of your beautiful songs would help."

Little Donkey just laughed. "Hee-haw!" he brayed. "Sing you a song? Oh, no! I'd rather sing to myself tonight." And he trotted away to the other side of the barn to sing a donkey song to himself.

"What a selfish little donkey!" bleated the sheep as she nestled down in the straw.

The next day, Little Donkey was taking a walk through the garden when he saw his friend the rabbit.

"Little Donkey, I have been trying to find some lunch for quite some time, but it seems that all the carrots in the garden have been pulled up. Would you mind sharing some of your lunch with me?" asked the rabbit. "I'm so very, very hungry."

"Hee-haw!" Little Donkey laughed. "Share my lunch? Oh, no! Then I wouldn't have enough for myself. Besides, I'd rather eat all by myself today."

"What a selfish little donkey!" said the rabbit. Then he hopped away.

After lunch, Little Donkey trotted over to a nearby field to take a nap. Before he could lie down, he heard the turtle calling.

"Little Donkey, will you please help me carry my house? It's too heavy for me to carry all the way down to the pond."

"Hee-haw!" Little Donkey snorted. "Help you carry your house? Oh, no! I was just about to take a nap." And he lay down and closed his eyes.

"What a selfish little donkey!" said the turtle as he lumbered away.

Later, the farmer loaded a pile of wood onto Little Donkey's back. Little Donkey had to carry the heavy load all the way to the house. He had gone just a short way when he saw his friend the sheep.

"Sheep, would you sing me a song?" Little Donkey asked. "I'd like to hear a cheerful tune while I'm carrying this load."

"Sing you a song?" bleated the sheep. "I remember asking you to sing me to sleep last night, and you laughed. Oh, no!" the sheep continued, "I'd rather sing to myself today."

There was nothing for Little Donkey to say, for he knew the sheep was right. He sadly continued on his way.

Farther on, Little Donkey saw the rabbit sniffing some grass.

"Rabbit, would you share your lunch with me?" he asked. "Carrying this wood has made me hungry."

"Share my lunch?" said the rabbit. "Oh, no! I'd rather eat all by myself today!"

Little Donkey felt like crying. No one wanted to help him, and he was getting more and more tired, and more and more hungry.

When Little Donkey reached the house at last, he saw the turtle.

"Turtle!" he called. "Would you help me unload some of this heavy wood? I don't know when the farmer will be here, and my back is hurting."

"Help you unload?" said the turtle. "Oh, no! You see, I was just about to take a nap." And with that, he plodded away.

Little Donkey waited until the farmer finally arrived and unloaded the wood. But the farmer was in such a hurry that he forgot to leave dinner for Little Donkey.

"That farmer thinks only of himself!" he said. "And because of that, I will have nothing to eat for dinner!"

Slowly it dawned on Little Donkey that he, too, had behaved selfishly toward all of his friends, and he began to cry.

The sheep, the rabbit, and the turtle heard Little Donkey crying. They led him into the barn, where the sheep sang him a sweet song, the rabbit fed him, and the turtle made him a soft bed of straw.

"I can't ever thank all of you enough," said Little Donkey. "Do you forgive me for being so selfish?"

"Of course we do," said the sheep kindly. "That's what friends are for."

"You're right," said Little Donkey. "And from now on, I'm going to make sure I'm a good friend to all of you—all the time."

Little Donkey laid his head down on the soft hay. Then he drifted off to sleep, dreaming about all the fun he would have with his friends tomorrow.

Donkeys can be almost any shade of gray or brown. They have big heads, long ears, and a dark stripe along their backs.

Donkeys are native to Africa and Asia, but they now live in dry areas all over the world.

Like horses, donkeys live on fresh grass, hay, and oats, but they will also eat dried grass and prickly thistles.